THE JELLY DONUT
DIFFERENCE
Sharing Kindness with the World

BY MARIA DISMONDY

ART BY P.S. BROOKS

Second Printing 2017
All rights reserved.
Printed in China
Summary: When a brother and sister just can't seem to get along, the friendship of an elderly neighbor and a recipe for jelly donuts change everything.

Dismondy, Maria Cini (1978-)
The Jelly Donut Difference: Sharing Kindness with the World
1. Acts of Kindness 2. Empathy 3. Family Life
4. Fiction 5. Relationships

ISBN: 978-0-9976085-0-2
LCCN: 2016943938

Cardinal Rule Press
An imprint of Maria Dismondy Inc.
5449 Sylvia
Dearborn Heights, MI 48125
www.cardinalrulepress.com

making spirits
bright

A portion of the proceeds from every sale of this book will be donated to Making Spirits Bright, a non-profit dedicated to helping children and families in need in the Metro Detroit area.

BEFORE READING:
⋆ Mention the title out loud. Talk to your child about what an act of kindness is.

⋆ Look at the cover illustration together.

⋆ Encourage your child to predict how jelly donuts can make a difference.

DURING READING:
⋆ Ask your child how they think Ms. Marvis feels having her family live far, far away.

⋆ The children made a batch of jelly donuts, ask your child to guess what might happen next.

⋆ Talk about the relationships you may have with your own neighbors. Explain the saying, "It takes a village" to your child.

AFTER:
⋆ Ask your child questions about the story.

⋆ How did the mama and papa show kindness?

⋆ How did Leah and Dexter show kindness? How can you show kindness to your neighbors?

ADDITIONAL LEARNING:
⋆ Come up with a plan to do 3 acts of kindness together as a family.

⋆ Take a field trip and visit a local bakery and try a jelly donut!

To our village of neighbors who share kindness and caring with our family. With special thanks to Dave and Hugh for your generosity.

M.D.

For my parents, sister and grandparents. Special thanks to Edward, Kate, Hannah and the rest of the Advocate Art team.

P.S.B.

The sun was barely up on this chilly winter morning when Dexter ran down the stairs, following the mouth-watering smell of his mom's famous bacon and cheese bread pudding.

"Not so fast!" Dexter's twin sister Leah yelled. She yanked his shirt, getting ahead of him in time to nab the first plate of their Saturday breakfast.

"Three weeks in a row, Dex!" Leah grinned, as she took the first bite of bacon-cheesy deliciousness.

"Why is it such a big deal to have the first bite of the pudding?" Dex demanded.

Mama and Papa were busy cooking for family and friends who would be coming to dinner that night.

"Leah, it's MY turn to mix the stuffing," Dexter said,
as he pulled the spoon right out of her hands.

It was then Papa realized they had run out of eggs. "Well, since you were the first to eat breakfast, Leah, you should go get eggs from Ms. Marvis," Dex told her.

Instead, Papa sent both kids to get the eggs from their neighbor.

Ms. Marvis answered the door and invited the twins inside. Right away, Dexter noticed a difference between their house and hers. It seemed too quiet. There were no good smells or messy countertops, just a bowl of cereal on the kitchen table. Dex wondered, *Where is Ms. Marvis's family? They never seem to come around.*

On the way home with the eggs, Dex turned to Leah, "Ms. Marvis's house seems so lonely."

"Our house is always full of people," Leah observed.

"So let's ask Mama and Papa to invite her over to dinner tonight," Dex suggested.

"Good idea," Leah agreed.

Ms. Marvis sat between Dex and Leah at the large dining table among other guests. She told stories of living in Poland with her children many years ago. She shared a Polish tradition of making and eating jelly donuts filled with sweet and savory fillings called pączki (pronounced POONCH-key). Dexter's eyes lit up!

Ms. Marvis told them, "Traditionally, we made pączki during the winter months to use up all the lard, sugar, eggs and fruit in the house before fasting for a holiday."

At the meal's end, Ms. Marvis thanked them all. "What a special treat to be here with you tonight! I love remembering when my children were young and the traditions we shared," Ms. Marvis said as she brushed away a tear. "Now they're grown and gone. Why, I haven't made those donuts in years!"

The next morning, the twins played in the snow. When they came in to warm up, Leah grabbed the last packet of hot cocoa mix right out of Dexter's hands.

Dex was about to yank back the mix when Papa interrupted. "I have a recipe here for pączki -- those jelly donuts Ms. Marvis mentioned. Do you want to make them with me?"

Soon the kitchen was filled with gooey blueberry filling, melted butter, whipping cream and other sticky ingredients. "Leah, it's your turn to stir," Dex said, trying not to lick sugar off his fingers as he handed his sister the spatula.

When they were done, the twins dropped off a
bag on Ms. Marvis's porch. "She'll love them. I just
know it," said Dex. He and Leah trudged back home
through the snow.

At dinner that night, the twins devoured jelly
donuts for dessert.

The following weekend, Dexter looked out the window. Leah was building a snowman! He ran out to join her.

Leah stepped in front of her snowman, "Stop, Dex, don't knock it down!"

"No, no, no, I wasn't going to," Dex replied. "I have an idea. Let's go build a snow family in Ms. Marvis's yard! She'll love all the company!"

A few days later on Monday, the twins found a letter from Ms. Marvis. Dex picked it up and read it out loud.

Dear Dexter and Leah,

The pączki you made for me were wonderful! Even better was the lovely dinner you invited me to and the snow family you built for me. Your acts of kindness are really appreciated. You found a great way to spend your time, and it made me feel extra special! Who would have thought jelly donuts could make such a difference?

Warm wishes,
Ms. Marvis

Before Leah could grab the letter from him, Dex handed it to her. "I'm thankful we have each other," he said. "It felt good to work together."

Leah grinned, "And I'm thankful we learned how to make jelly donuts!"

The twins giggled until their bellies hurt, thinking about the new treats and tradition they hoped to continue.

TIPS TO HELP YOUR FAMILY
Share Kindness with the World

* **KINDNESS IN THE FAMILY COMES FIRST.** Try to model kindness as a parent. From your tone of voice to expressing love and gratitude, all of this counts in building kindness in the family.

* **INTEGRATE KINDNESS INTO YOUR DAILY HABITS.** From reading books at bedtime about kindness, to having dinner conversations focused on how we were kind to others, we teach our kids how to live a kindness lifestyle.

* **LITTLE ACTS OF KINDNESS ARE POWERFUL.** Small, frequent acts of kindness become more powerful tools in changing behavior and creating lasting kindness habits.

* **ALONG THE WAY, SLOW DOWN THE PACE.** Kids need time to recognize need, see how they can help, and then act on those feelings.

* **HONOR YOUR CHILDREN'S PERSONALITIES AS THEY LEARN TO BE KIND.** Your children will each approach helping someone in different ways. That is the way it should be, and I encourage you to embrace that.

*Sheila Sjolseth believes that teaching kids to be kind results in a happier family. What started as a way to teach her kids empathy has transitioned to a way of life and a connection with thousands of others. Now, as the President and Founder of **Pennies of Time: Teach Kids to Serve**, her goal is for families to choose to complete an act of kindness as often as they go to soccer practice or to the movies. Sheila earned her Masters from the Harvard Graduate School of Education.*

Award-winning author, Maria Dismondy inspires lives through her poignant stories about topics challenging today's modern child. Maria's background in early education and commitment to teach the importance of character building enables her to touch lives the world over while touring as a public speaker in schools, community forums, and at national conferences. Maria's eighth book, *The Jelly Donut Difference*, drives home the important message of generosity and kindness. She included the Polish donuts as a nod to her heritage. When Maria isn't writing, she can be found embarking on adventures throughout southeast Michigan and beyond, where she lives with her husband and three book-loving children.

P.S. Brooks is a YA writer and children's illustrator based in Yorkshire, UK. He is a graduate in Fine Art and works primarily in Photoshop using scanned textures such as pastels, paints and other media. He has worked in video games and enjoys connecting with other writers and illustrators online. When not illustrating or writing, he likes to watch fantasy and sci-fi movies and shows, and also plays with his Sheltie guinea pigs Little Jupiter and Big Jupiter.